the MiSADV...

MiCHAEL McMiCHAELS

vol. 5

The Case of the Escaping Elephants

by **Tony Penn**
illustrated by **Brian Martin**

BOYS TOWN® Press

Boys Town, Nebraska

BOYS TOWN® Press

For a Boys Town Press catalog, call 1-800-282-6657
or visit our website: BoysTownPress.org

Publisher's Cataloging-in-Publication Data

Names: Penn, Tony, 1973-, author. | Martin, Brian (Brian Michael), 1978- illustrator.

Title: The case of the escaping elephants / by Tony Penn ; illustrated by Brian Martin.

Description: Boys Town, NE : Boys Town Press, [2018] | Series: The misadventures
of Michael McMichaels ; vol. 5. | Audience: grades 2-6. | Summary: Michael
McMichaels' obsession with video games leads to rampaging elephants and a guilty
conscience. Will this messy misadventure cure his addiction to electronics and scare
him into limiting his screen time? It's a humorous tale about the importance of
moderation.--Publisher.

Identifiers: ISBN: 978-1-944882-32-7

Subjects: LCSH: Video game addiction--Juvenile fiction. | Video games and children-
-Juvenile fiction. | Internet addiction--Juvenile fiction. | Electronic apparatus and
appliances--Psychological aspects--Juvenile fiction. | Compulsive behavior--Juvenile
fiction. | Moderation--Juvenile fiction. | Friendship--Juvenile fiction. | Behavior--
Juvenile fiction. | Interpersonal relations in children--Juvenile fiction. | Children-
-Life skills guides. | CYAC: Video games--Fiction. | Internet addiction--Fiction. |
Electronic apparatus and appliances--Fiction. | Compulsive behavior--Fiction. |
Moderation--Fiction. | Friendship--Fiction. | Behavior--Fiction. | Interpersonal
relations--Fiction. | Conduct of life. | BISAC: JUVENILE FICTION / Readers /
Chapter Books. | JUVENILE FICTION / Social Themes / Manners & Etiquette.
| JUVENILE FICTION / Comics & Graphic Novels / Humorous. | JUVENILE
FICTION / Social Themes / Friendship. | JUVENILE NONFICTION / Readers /
Chapter Books. | JUVENILE NONFICTION / Social Topics / Manners & Etiquette.

Classification: LCC: PZ7.1.P44718 M4725 2018 | DDC: [Fic]--dc23

10 9 8 7 6 5 4 3 2 1

Boys Town Press is the publishing division of
Boys Town, a national organization serving
children and families.

*For all my friends,
near and far, from Marissa
on the seesaw in the
Bronx, to you, reader,
wherever you are*

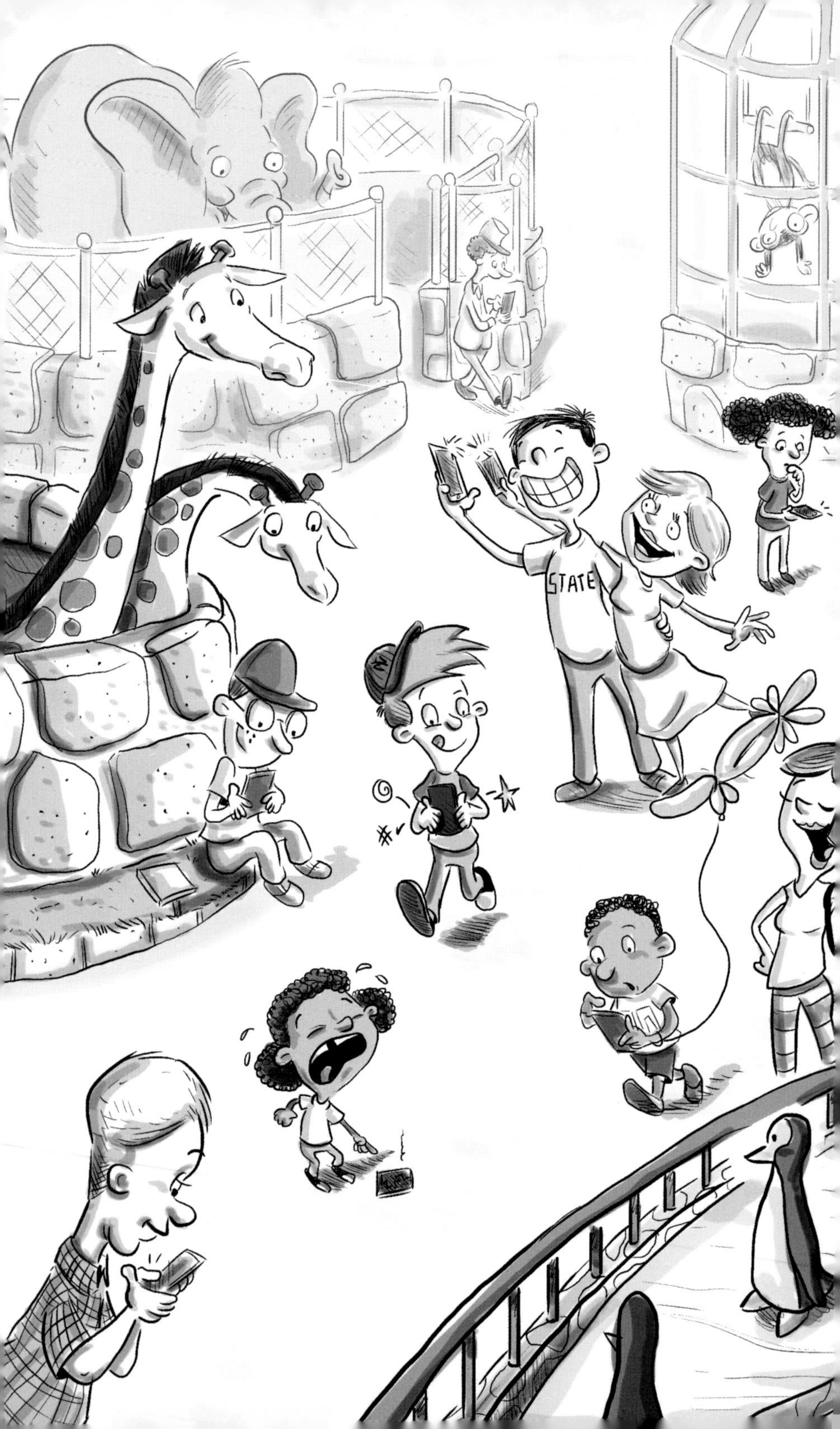
STATE

Chapter 1

You're not going to believe the mess I got myself into this time. My life stinks! It stinks worse than the zoo in July. Why doesn't someone invent a toilet for those animals, or maybe a giant air freshener so we all don't have to pinch our noses and say, 'Eww, gross!' so many times? And why doesn't someone else invent clothes for those animals, too? At least underwear. I get embarrassed when everyone is staring at a buffalo's butt or a tiger's tush.

Anyway, like I was saying, my life stinks and this time it's bad. I mean really bad. It's kind of a complicated story, but it all started on a Sunday at the zoo with my family. It was a beautiful day and

1

lots of people were there. I was getting hungry so I asked my father where we were going to eat. He said he didn't know where the food stand was, so he handed me his cell phone and told me to look it up on the zoo's website. I looked around and noticed almost every adult was looking down at a phone more than at the animals.

I can't say I blame them. **I LOVE cell phones and borrow my parents' phones whenever I get a chance. They are so much fun!** The games are great and you can just keep playing and playing. I wish I had my own phone, but I'm too young. My parents said I can get one when I finish fifth grade, which is in a million years. Ok, more like two years, but you know what I mean.

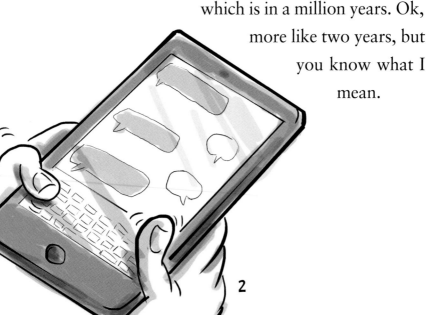

2

After I found out where the food stand was, I started playing a game on my dad's phone called CASTLES! You have to build castles using blocks and you're always racing someone. It's fun. I logged in under my account and saw my mom's friend's son, Jimmy, who's in college, was online and I began to play him. I won, and right after the match he sent me a message and said he liked the Yankees cap I was wearing. I screamed because I thought he could see through the phone. **Could he see that I just picked my nose, too?**

It turned out he was working at the elephant sanctuary and he saw me and my family as we were walking around. He sent another message saying he really should get back to work, but I begged him to play a few more rounds with me. He said no, but I really wanted him to keep playing.

I got an idea and sent him a message: "Hey, Jimmy, how does it feel losing to a third grader? If I lost to someone so young, I would be **SO EMBARRASSED."**

He still said no.

Then I got another idea.

"You know my cousin, Mary, the really pretty one, who goes to college?" I texted. "Well, I'll tell her you were nice enough to keep playing with me, even though I'm just a kid, and you were super busy. She is always talking about liking nice guys. I'm sure she'll be impressed by THAT!"

He agreed to keep playing. **YES!!!**

We played and played and played, even though my mother kept telling me to focus on the animals and to stop distracting Jimmy while he was at work. Finally, it must have been too much, because Dad took his phone back and did not seem very pleased. But that was fine because we found that food stand and I was really hungry! We went home not long after that. Sounds good, right?

Well, you're never going to believe what happened next, but it's true. I swear on a whole pie of pepperoni pizza. My friend, Kenny, came over to my house later that day. He ate dinner with us and then we went outside to play hide-and-seek. I was hiding behind a tree when I heard a loud stomping noise. It sounded like thunder or something, but I looked up and the sky was clear. It was getting dark, but there wasn't a cloud in the sky. The noise got louder. I heard police sirens and saw a helicopter flying up above. I started to get nervous, then Kenny crept around the tree I was hiding behind.

"Ha, found you!" he said.

"Ok, now you hide," I said.

Kenny's eyes bugged out and he screamed,

"UGH, Mikey, look!"

I turned around to face the street and then I saw it… a giant elephant charging down the street and trumpeting like crazy.

"I need my inhaler, Mikey!" Kenny said.

"Call 911! Call the FBI! Call Ellen – she loves animals!"

I screamed, as the elephant charged past us. Kenny fainted on the grass, but by then my whole family and everyone else on the block were outside on their front lawns.

Nobody seemed to know how to stop a charging elephant. **Do you?**

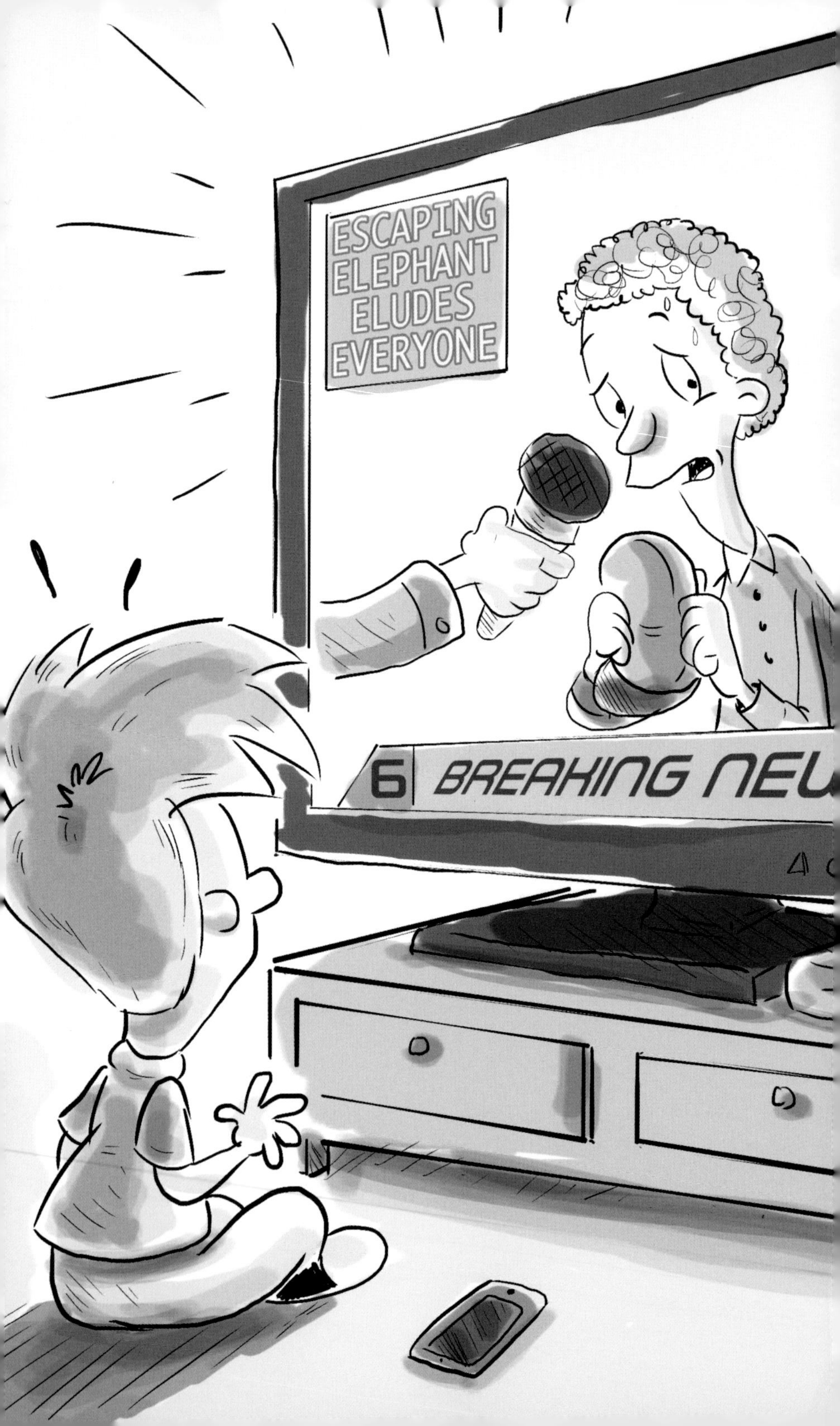
ESCAPING ELEPHANT ELUDES EVERYONE
6
BREAKING NEW

Chapter 2

"Wake up, Kenny, wake up!"
I yelled, then smacked him in the face to see if that
would work. People do that on TV, so I figured it
was acceptable.

"Don't hurt him!" my mother said, "I have an
idea." Then she leaned over Kenny and turned her
water bottle upside down right onto his face.

That woke him up really fast.

"There's a flood! Call the navy! Get my goggles!" he cried.

"There's no flood," I said. "You just fainted,
that's all."

"Oh, what a relief, phew," he said, standing up.
"I had the craziest dream that an elephant charged
down the street. Then the next thing I knew,

someone was beating me up. Then it rained."
He looked very confused.

"Ah, yeah, terrible dream," I said. "Except there actually WAS an elephant charging down our block. But the other stuff, yeah, it sounds like you really were dreaming."

"THERE WAS AN ELEPHANT CHARGING DOWN THE BLOCK?" Kenny screamed.

"Yes, he's on his way back to the zoo now. They were able to catch him a few minutes ago and put him in a special van," my father said. "Everyone, let's go inside now and watch the local news to see what really happened. It's funny that we were just at the zoo looking at the elephants a few hours ago."

The reporter said four elephants escaped from the zoo, but only three had been found. The fourth, a young female, was still on the loose!

"How in the world can they not find an elephant?" my mother said. "That's crazy!"

"Listen up!" my father said. "She's explaining now." He turned up the volume on the TV.

"The town did not have enough fire trucks, police cars, and helicopters to chase four elephants at once," the reporter said. "Now that three have been found, all of the town's resources are currently being devoted to finding the last escaped elephant. If anyone in the community spots her, please call 911 right away. It seems as though the gate of the elephant sanctuary was left unlocked by accident. Here to comment on that is zoo intern, Jimmy Gorton."

Then my game-playing buddy Jimmy came on and looked really upset. He said he was distracted using his cell phone and forgot to lock up. He apologized and looked really sad.

"Oh, that's Camille's son!" my mother said. "I'd better go call her. He must feel terrible."

OH NO! Jimmy was playing CASTLES! on his phone with ME when this happened! He wanted to stop to focus on his work with the elephants, but I begged him and even involved my cousin, Mary, to keep him playing. We even played after I came home. That's when he was supposed to be locking up, so it was my fault, too! My heart was racing so fast I couldn't believe it. What if they found out I was the reason he was distracted on his cell phone?

I grabbed Kenny by the wrist, dragged him down to my basement and told him everything.

"Mikey, you did it again! Why can't you stay out of trouble for like one whole month?" Kenny asked.

"Don't ask me things like that right now!" I said. "I'm getting nervous. I can barely breathe! They're going to arrest me now. It's my fault..."

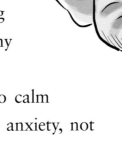

"Mikey, you need to calm down. I'm the one with anxiety, not you," Kenny said.

"Yeah, well, you're not the one who is responsible for those elephants escaping from the zoo. That's my fault," I said.

"Good point. It IS your fault," Kenny agreed.

"STOP THAT!" I said. "You're my friend. You're supposed to comfort me."

"Well, it's Jimmy's fault, too," Kenny said. "But you told him you would tell your cousin, Mary, he was nice to little kids. I'm sure that was a big reason he kept playing."

"Ok, you're not helping!" I cried.

Kenny went home a little while later. I watched some TV with my family then went to bed. Only I couldn't sleep because that elephant was still missing, even at the end of the night, and it was

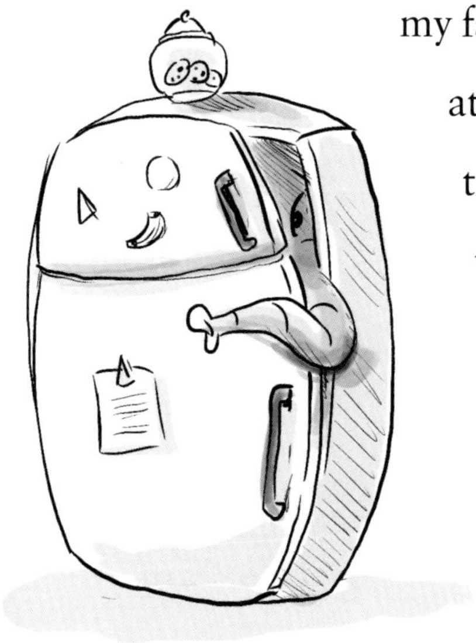

my fault. What would the people at the zoo do to me now that this was the SECOND bad thing I'd done there, including the *Angry Alligator* incident? But, really, I didn't mean to.

"Where could an elephant hide?" I thought. I stared at my ceiling and tried to go to sleep.

Behind a tree? **No.**

In someone's fridge? **No.**

In a restaurant bathroom? **No.**

In a car? **No.**

Under a kid's bed? **No...** And even though I knew she couldn't be there, I leaned my head over the side of the bed to check.

Phew! All clear.

Where would I go if I was an elephant? Hmmmm...

Then it came to me.

Someone's pool! I'd go in a backyard pool because elephants love water.

I sprang out of bed, ran downstairs in my Christmas-tree pajama bottoms and opened the patio sliding door to check the pool.

But the alarm went off. I forgot about that!

When my parents came downstairs, I told them I thought the elephant could be in our pool.

"Go right to bed!" they both said at the same time, like they had practiced it.

"All right, all right," I said. But they didn't know it was my fault, and I just had to find that elephant.

But how do you find a missing elephant?

Any ideas?

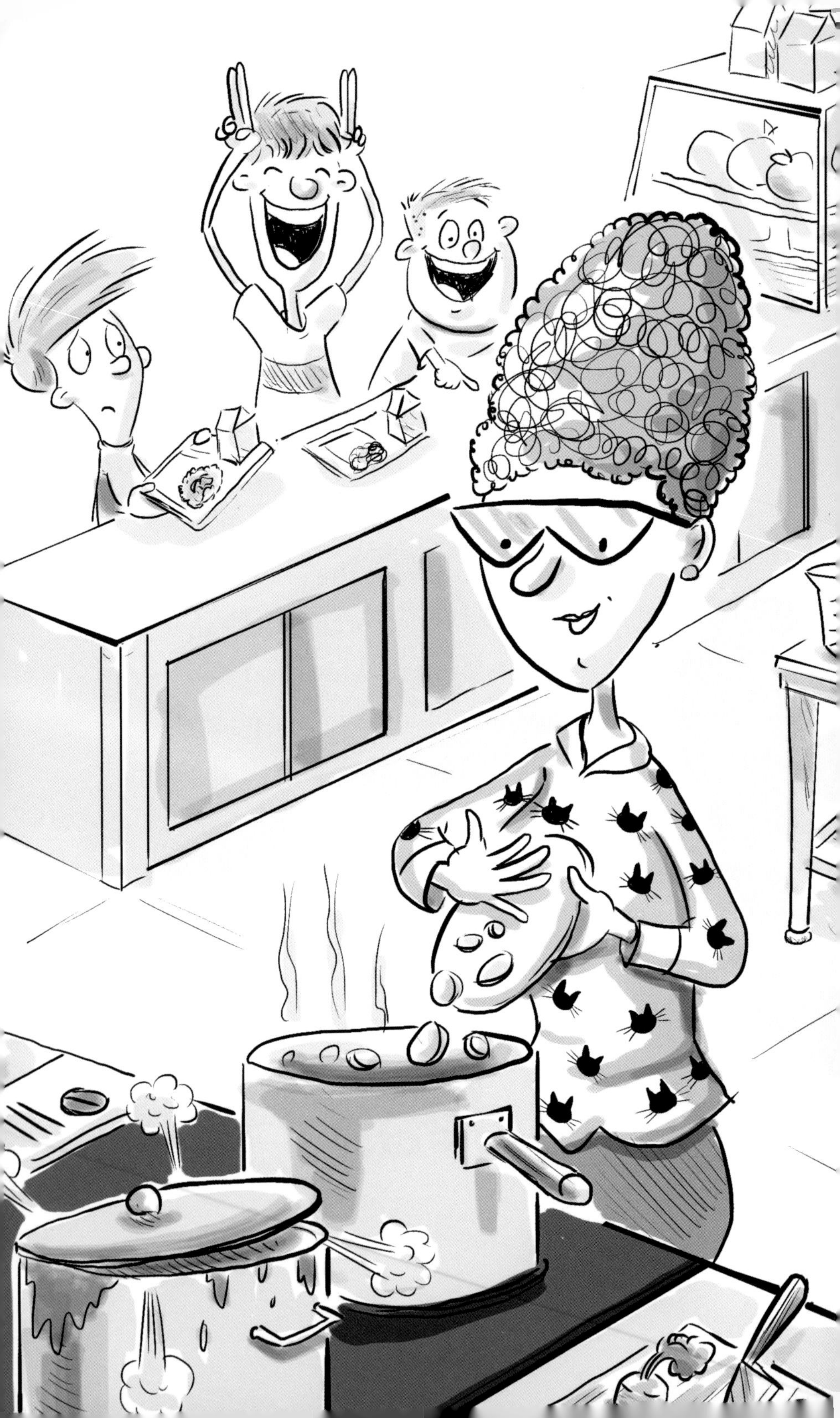

Chapter 3

Everyone was talking about the missing elephant the next day at school. One kid said he thought she ran to China. I wanted to say that's not possible from America, but I was afraid to be called a nerd. I love maps, but no one else does, I guess. Another kid said she must have gone home to visit her family. Maybe in Africa. Or maybe at Animal Kingdom in Florida.

Everywhere I went, I looked over my shoulder expecting to see the elephant.

Under my seat in the school bus.

In my book bag.

In my pencil case.

I knew it would come out that it was my fault. I also knew I should say something to someone, but that made me SO nervous. They'll find that elephant soon, I said to myself as I got into the lunch line at the cafeteria.

I was tired because I didn't sleep much. I thought I would be arrested in my sleep for being part of the elephants' escape.

I was hoping they were serving something good like tacos or pizza, but they were serving fish sticks. Yuck! Oh well. I heard a couple of fifth-graders ahead of me giggling about the way the new lunch lady, Ms. Fox, looked. She wore old-fashioned glasses that made her look like a giant bug. And she always wore clothes with animals on them. Today, it was kittens. Maybe a hundred of them climbing all over her. She had a weird hairstyle that made it look like she was balancing a pineapple on her head. My mother said women used to wear their hair like that many years ago. Ms. Fox didn't realize, I guess, she was the only one still doing it.

"Hey, look at her!" one kid said. "What a freak! The circus is in town. She must work there, too!"

"She probably got those glasses on sale for fifty cents at the Dollar Store!" another kid said, cracking up.

I felt bad for her and wanted to stop those kids, but they were older and bigger. The good news was Ms. Fox couldn't hear them.

After my gym class, I was headed to the locker room to change when I heard a helicopter overhead. Was it the police? The FBI? Were they coming for me? How many years do you have to spend in jail for causing an elephant to escape from a zoo and then go missing? The helicopter went past my school. Whew. It was probably still searching for the missing elephant.

Where could she be?

We always have to hurry in the locker room because the fifth-graders are in gym right after us. So, I wasn't surprised when I looked across the room and saw Erik, the fifth-grader who I had a problem with in the *Angry Alligator* book. What did surprise me was he was smirking at me like he knew something. Something BIG. Some kind of secret!

Oh no! What if he knew it was my fault the

elephants escaped? What if he knew I begged Jimmy Gorton to keep playing the game, even though he wanted to stop? What if he knew I even called Jimmy a loser for losing to a third-grader, and promised to say good things about him to my cousin? And what if he plans to tell everyone it was my fault?

I hurried up and got out of there as fast as I could.

I've GOT to figure this out! I need to do whatever it takes to find that elephant or this guilt is going to eat me alive? (I wonder what that expression really means. I mean, it's not like guilt is an actual body or something that COULD eat you – dead or alive. But I've heard a lot of people use that expression, so I figured it must apply here.)

Anyway, I was trying to figure out how to find the elephant. Of course I could ask Kenny, he's my best friend. He can't say no to me. But can we do this by ourselves? We probably need someone who's pretty smart, especially someone who adults will listen to. And as much as

I hate to say it, that might mean working with my arch enemy – Harriet.

But Harriet is such a **BIG MOUTH!** How will I possibly convince her to work with us AND keep it a secret?

Ugh. I can't imagine. But I'll think about it and decide.

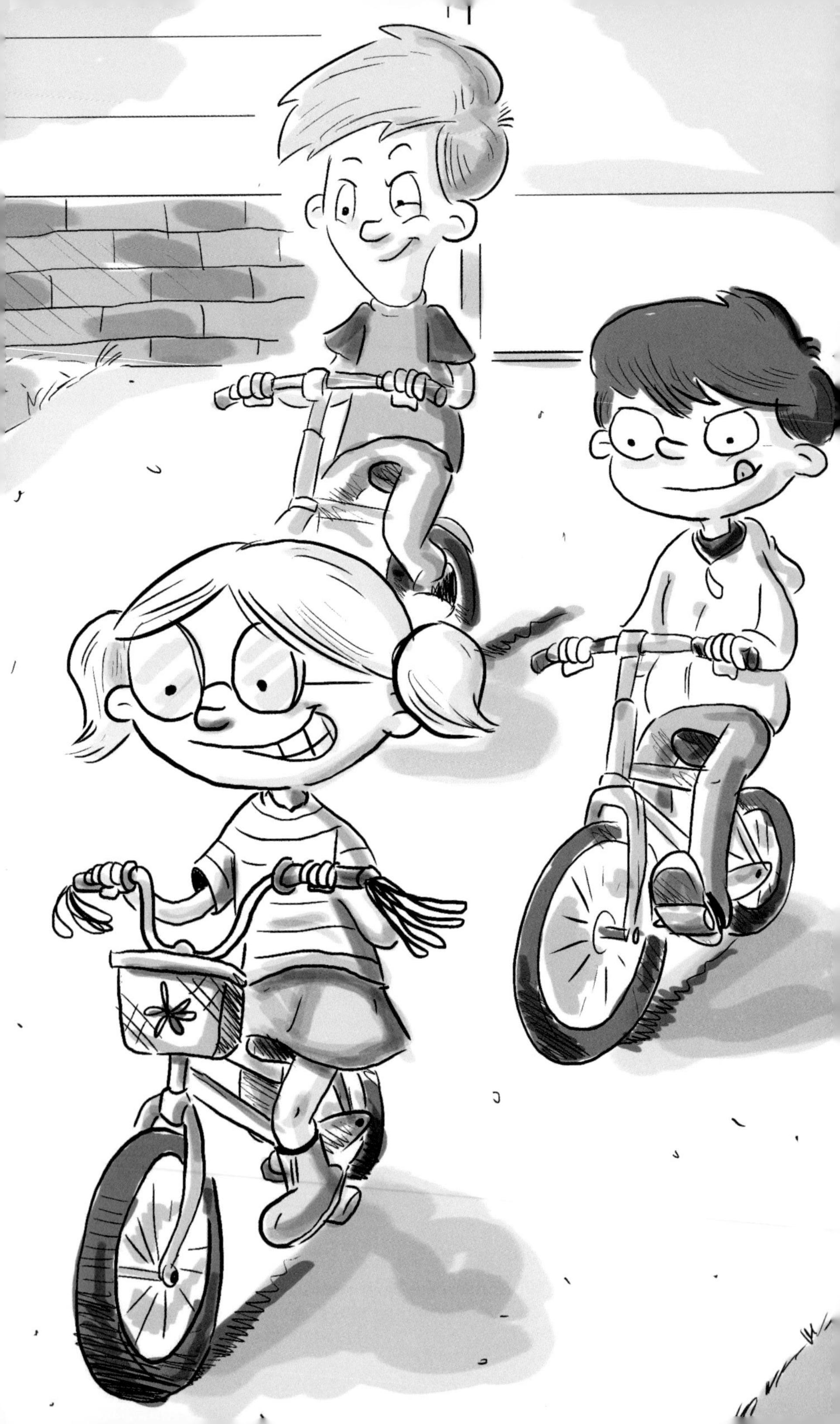

Chapter 4

After dinner, I asked my mother if I could borrow her iPad. That's another thing I have to wait a few years to get. It stinks being young, but it really doesn't matter much when your parents let you borrow their technology all the time. She was using her phone, so she said it was ok for me to use her iPad. I've noticed lately that my parents and most adults are on their phones A LOT.

I logged in and began to play my cousin, Tommy, when I got a message. It was from Jimmy Gorton!

"Hey, Michael. So, it stinks this elephant is still missing, right?" Jimmy texted.

"Oh, yeah. It stinks worse than my father's

23

feet. Worse than old milk. Worse than the garbage with a baby's diaper in it," I typed.

"Well, whatever. It's both our faults. You begged me to continue playing, and I agreed. I also kept playing with my other friend after you left. Have you told anyone yet?" he asked.

"No, I haven't. Have you?" I said.

"Well, I told a few people, but they are trustworthy," he replied. "Maybe they'd find the elephant if

there was a reward or something?"

Wait. What if Jimmy DID tell Erik? And if Erik knows, he might really tell someone, and then I'm **sunk!**

"Anyway, Jimmy, I have to go now. Let's cross our fingers they find the elephant soon," I said.

"Yeah, you probably don't want to be on the news like I was. I got fired from the zoo because of it," he typed.

"Oh, no. That's terrible," I said.

"Yeah, but I'm going to do something to prove I'm sorry and a good worker. Don't know what that is yet. So, did you get a chance to tell your cousin, Mary, about me?" he asked.

"Not yet. She's on vacation in a place where they don't have cellphones. Neptune, I think. Gotta go! Later!" I texted back.

It really did stink he got fired from the zoo, but I had to get back to my game with my cousin. I think my parents called me when I was playing, but I ignored them. I wanted to **WIN, WIN, WIN!**

"Michael," my mother said loudly, standing right next to me. "Your friends are at the door. They want you to go outside and ride your bike with them."

Oops, I forgot about that. We had to look

for the elephant. I had told Kenny and Harriet to come to my house for a top-secret mission.

"Oh yeah! I'm coming, Mom," I said, turning off the iPad.

"Promise me you won't go more than two blocks away. And be careful. Make sure to ride on the sidewalk and cross only after looking both ways. You promise?" she asked.

I promised, and then I hopped on my bike and met up with Kenny and Harriet outside my house. I knew we would be going far, but I couldn't tell my mother that. I didn't like lying to her, but this was serious. I didn't think I had a choice!

"Ok, McMichaels, spill it. Why did you tell us to meet you here?" Harriet said. She did not look happy.

"Yeah," Kenny said and sneezed. "My allergies are acting up and I don't want you to get us in trouble again. My nerves can't take it. What are you up to?"

"I'm not up to anything," I said. "I just need your help to find the elephant."

"Why us?" They both asked at the same time.

I wanted to tell them the truth, but I was too scared. "Because you are the smartest kids I know. And because if we can crack the case we will be famous and they will have a parade for us on Main Street."

"I have always wanted a parade," Harriet said, running her fingers through her hair. "And I do love solving crimes. You know I've read all of the *Nancy Drew* books even though they are for older kids?"

"Yeah, and I feel bad for that elephant," Kenny said. "But how can we find her if the police can't? We're just kids."

"Yeah, but every famous person started out as a kid. We can do it!" I said.

"Hold it right there, Mister!" Harriet said. "First of all, you have to agree to follow my instructions if we are going to work as a team. I am in charge. Second, you have to agree to use my basement as the command center – I have all kinds of cool stuff down there. And third, you must turn your t-shirt right side out. I cannot be seen around here with a slob who cannot even put his shirt on the right way!"

I looked down, and sure enough, my shirt was on inside out. Probably happened after gym class. I wonder if that's what Erik was grinning about earlier? Figures. But I can't risk it – maybe he DOES know, and maybe he WILL tell if we don't find this elephant soon enough!

So I agreed to Harriet's terms, and she turned her back so I could put my shirt on the right way in private. Then off we went to the command center – Harriet's basement.

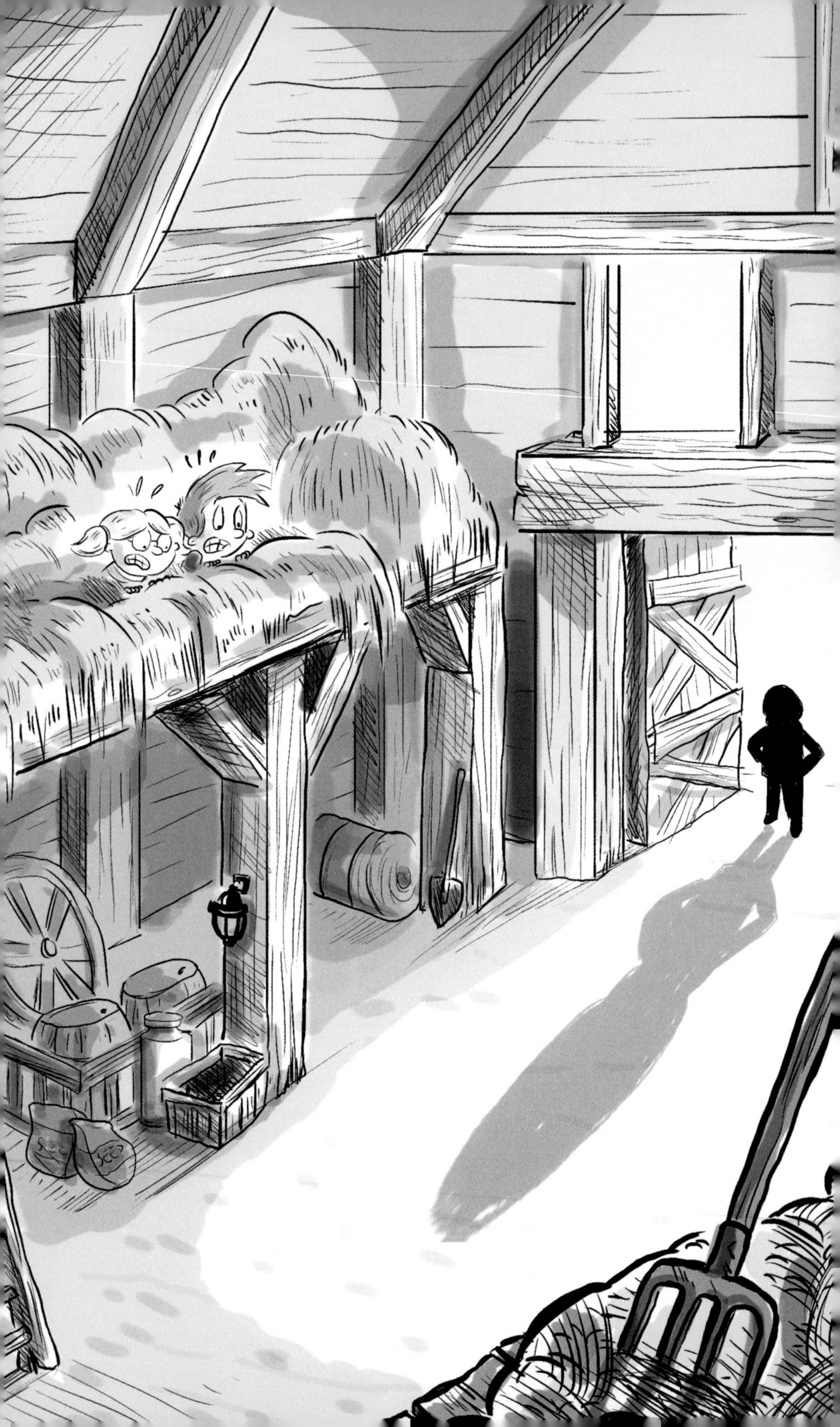

Chapter 5

Harriet's basement was really cool. There were all kinds of toys, books, and even her brother's virtual reality system.

"Guys, I have an idea!" I said. "Let's use the virtual reality machine to look for the elephant."

Kenny and Harriet agreed.

We each put on these really funky goggles, turned the system on, and all of a sudden, we were flying through space.

"Let's go to Africa," Kenny said. "The elephant will probably be there."

The next thing we knew, we were flying over the Sahara Desert toward the pyramids.

"This is fabulous!" Harriet said. "I was Cleopatra for Halloween a few years ago. I know deep down inside that I am a queen, so I can relate to her."

"Ooh, look!" I said. "There's the sphinx." That's a giant statue in the desert with the head of a man and the body of a lion. I learned in social studies class there is a riddle you can ask, and it may even answer.

"Hey, guys, let's virtual reality (or VR as I like to call it) down in front of the sphinx so we can ask it where the elephant is."

It was crazy, but it really felt like we were there

in the desert. It was hot and the pyramids were in the distance. It even felt like we were standing in sand.

"Ok, sphinx," I said. "I know I can ask you for advice, so here's the question: There's a missing elephant that escaped from the zoo here in town. Can you tell us where she is?"

Harriet, Kenny, and I all went totally silent as we waited for the answer.

"Put those goggles down right now and use your minds. Technology is not the answer! Plus, it belongs to me!" the sphinx said.

"Ugh! It's talking to us," Harriet screamed. "I'm triggered!"

Just then I turned around and saw Harriet's older brother, Sam, standing there. "Give me those goggles!" he said. "They're mine!"

It turns out it wasn't the sphinx talking to us after all. It was Sam. But he had a good point. Technology isn't the answer. We should use our minds.

"But where could she be?" Kenny said. "I have no idea."

"Let's see," I said. "If someone is holding her, she'd have to eat. What do elephants eat?"

"Peanuts!" Harriet said.

"Exactly!" I said.

"I have an idea where that elephant is hiding," I whispered. Everyone leaned in to hear. "She's probably at Carter's Peanut Farm. I know I'd go there if I was an elephant."

"Why?" Kenny asked.

"Because elephants love peanuts, you ding-a-ling!" I shot back.

"Well, they can also get those at the supermarket," Kenny said. "Aisle 6, I think. Or is it 8?"

"Something like that," I said. "Everyone, follow me."

We all rode our bikes really fast – on the sidewalks, of course – to Carter's Peanut Farm. I got scared a couple of times because on the main road there were big trucks going by. Now I know why my mother told me not to go this far. It's dangerous! I shouldn't have lied to her, but I thought I had to find the elephant.

We got to the farm and hid our bikes behind a big tree. Then we all jumped over a low fence and into the rows of growing peanuts.

"It smells like peanut butter here," Kenny said. "Where's the jelly farm? They should be together, right?"

"No, no, no, you silly, silly boy," Harriet said. "You don't pay attention in class, I can tell. Jelly is made from grapes. It doesn't grow directly from the ground in jars."

"Oh, that's boring," Kenny said.

"You guys need to hush up," I said. "We don't want Mr. Carter to hear us walking around his farm. Besides, I think I know where the elephant is." I pointed to a barn in the distance. "She must be in there. Let's go!"

I have to admit, I was scared. I mean, what if she wasn't there and instead there were bats flying around. Or lions. Or tigers. Or…

We crept up to the barn and put our ears up to it.

Silence.

"She's probably sleeping," I said. "But let's check it out anyway."

All three of us together had to lift a large wood beam blocking the barn door and then we were able to enter. The place was so quiet, I could hear my breath and my heart beating.

"I don't see an elephant," Kenny said. "Guess it's time to go home."

I could tell he was super nervous, too.

"Not yet," I said, pointing. "She might be sleeping under that hay."

We began to dive into the hay, throwing it everywhere. There was no elephant there, but it was kind of fun jumping around in the hay like that. I even lost track of where Kenny and Harriet were.

A few minutes later we heard a noise. It was the barn door opening slowly.

Harriet screamed. "Oh, no. It's the army! I can't be arrested. If I am, Prince George will never marry me. A royal can never marry a common criminal."

"It's the FBI and the police!" a voice said. I thought I recognized it, but the voice was very deep so it couldn't be a kid.

"We're looking for the elephant," I said. "We thought she'd be near peanuts." I looked around but couldn't find Kenny.

"Arrest THEM, FBI and the police!"

Harriet said with her English accent. "But please don't arrest me. I CAN'T have a record. I just CAN'T."

Her "can't" sounded like "kont" with her accent, which I have to admit sometimes sounds really good. I'm actually kind of jealous.

"We are waiting for some other officers to arrive" the voice said. "They're on their way **TO ARREST YOU!**"

"OH NO!" I screamed. I couldn't be arrested either! I began to get dizzy and the next thing I knew, Harriet was helping me get up from the floor. I had fainted.

Then the barn door opened all the way. It was Kenny playing a trick on us with a fake deep voice. He wouldn't stop laughing.

As we biked home, I got nervous thinking my parents would find out I disobeyed them and rode to the other side of town. I shouldn't do things like this, but sometimes I can't help myself.

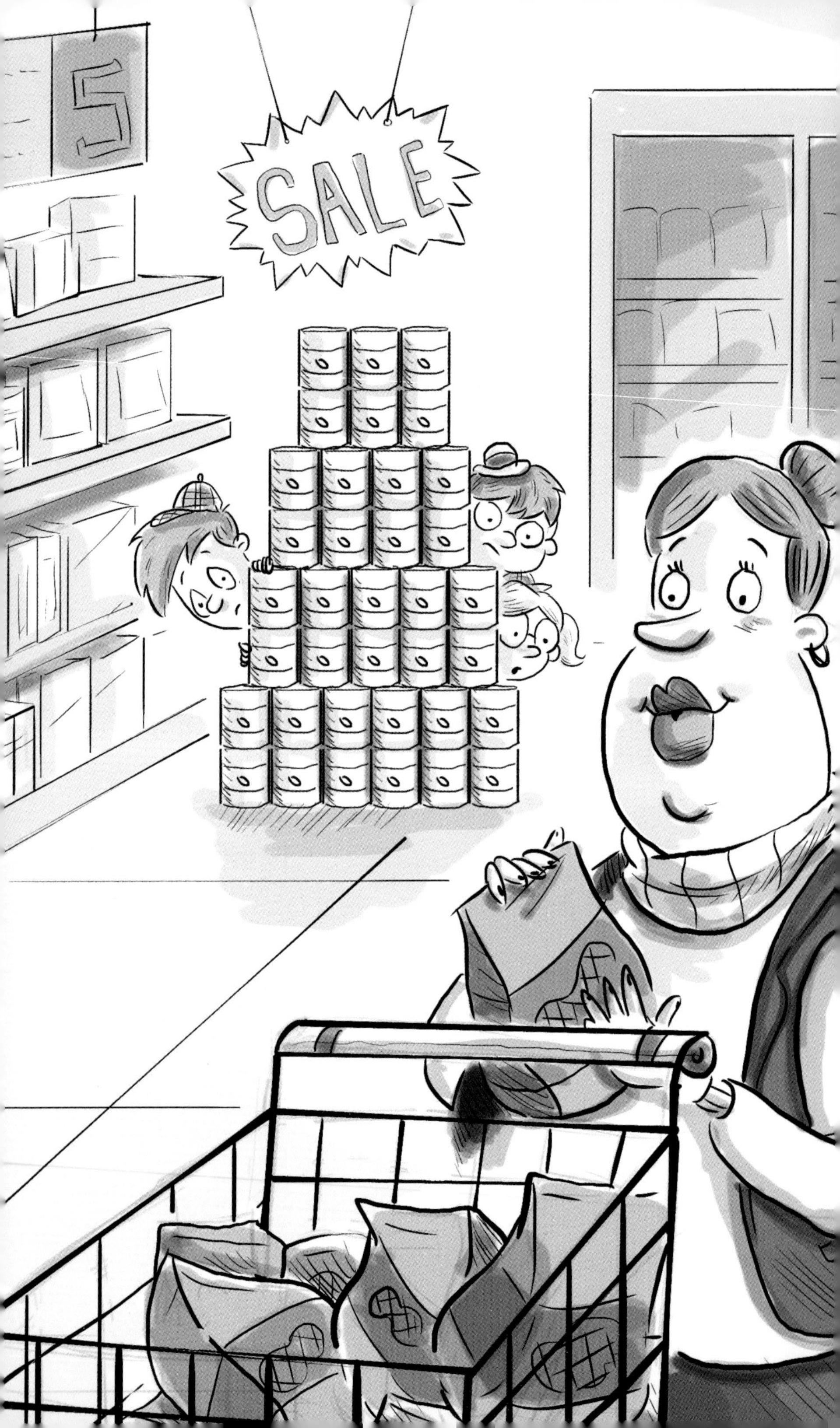
5
SALE

Chapter 6

The next day after school, I lied to my parents again and said I was going to Kenny's house to do homework. Instead, Kenny, Harriet, and I were going to do more investigating. We met in Harriet's basement, our command center.

"Ok, so lucky for you guys my mother got us costumes we can use to conduct our investigations. She works at the local theater and you two will be Sherlock and Watson. Here are your costumes. Aren't you excited?"

We had no choice. When Harriet gets an idea in her head, that's that. Kenny and I changed into our costumes and Harriet changed into hers.

"Who are you, Harriet?" I asked.

"I'm Miss Marple, another famous British investigator," she said. "Now we have a better chance to solve this mystery, because when you're dressed properly, you are halfway there."

I had a thought.

"Yesterday when Kenny said we can find peanuts in aisle 6 of the supermarket, we laughed. But I think he was onto something," I said, pacing back and forth, looking through my magnifying glass.

"That the elephant is living in the supermarket?" Kenny asked.

"No! If someone is keeping the elephant at their house, they will have to buy a ton of peanuts to feed her!" I said.

"So, what are you saying?" Harriet asked.

"I'm saying we should stake out the peanut aisle of the supermarket and see who buys a lot of peanuts!"

Kenny and Harriet thought that was a great idea. Harriet even asked her mother when she'd be going to the supermarket. It turned out she was going there that night. She agreed to take us.

While Harriet's mother was shopping, the

three of us stood near the peanuts waiting to see who bought a lot of them. We were all in costume. I was looking through my magnifying glass, Kenny had his pad out, and Harriet had a make-up brush and some of her mother's eye shadow, ready to dust for fingerprints.

For some reason, every time someone walked past us they stared and made a strange face. They acted like they never saw three kids dressed up like detectives doing an official investigation in the supermarket or something!

Two people bought a jar of peanuts and one person even bought a bag. We decided that wasn't enough, so we didn't do an investigation into them. Harriet's mother was in line buying her groceries so we knew we didn't have much time left.

Then it happened!

Mrs. Wiggins, the librarian, bought five big bags of peanuts. As she put them in her shopping cart, Kenny, Harriet, and I approached her. For some reason she looked concerned.

We were about to question her when Harriet's mother had us paged over the loudspeaker to meet her at the front of the store. She had finished shopping. We had to move quickly, so we didn't get to ask Miss Wiggins anything.

Back at our command center in Harriet's basement, we talked about our next move.

"So, now we have to question Mrs. Wiggins, that's for sure," I said.

"But what if that doesn't work out?" Harriet said. "We have to have another plan."

"Yeah, the news said the last place the missing elephant was spotted was on Pine Drive. There are only three houses there, right?" Kenny said. "That's just one street over from my house."

"Yeah, who lives in those three houses?" I asked.

Harriet hopped onto the Internet and looked it up. **"OH, MY WORD!"** she cried. "Guess who lives there? You'll never believe it."

"Beyoncé?" Kenny asked.

Harriet shot him a look like he was crazy.

"What?" he said. "You said we'd never believe it so...."

"Well, Sherlock and Watson," Harriet said

to me and Kenny, "Mrs. Wiggins lives there, and so does the Smalls family. Their kids go to our school."

"Ugh! And he's a hunter," I said. "We have to interview him, too."

"Who is the third person who lives there, Harriet?" Kenny asked.

"The third house is empty. It's the house that rich kid Zeke's family bought but then abandoned."

"Well, we have to check all of them out," I said. "Let's all meet again tomorrow after school at Kenny's house."

"Yeah," Kenny said. "We can do this! And we'll even be famous!"

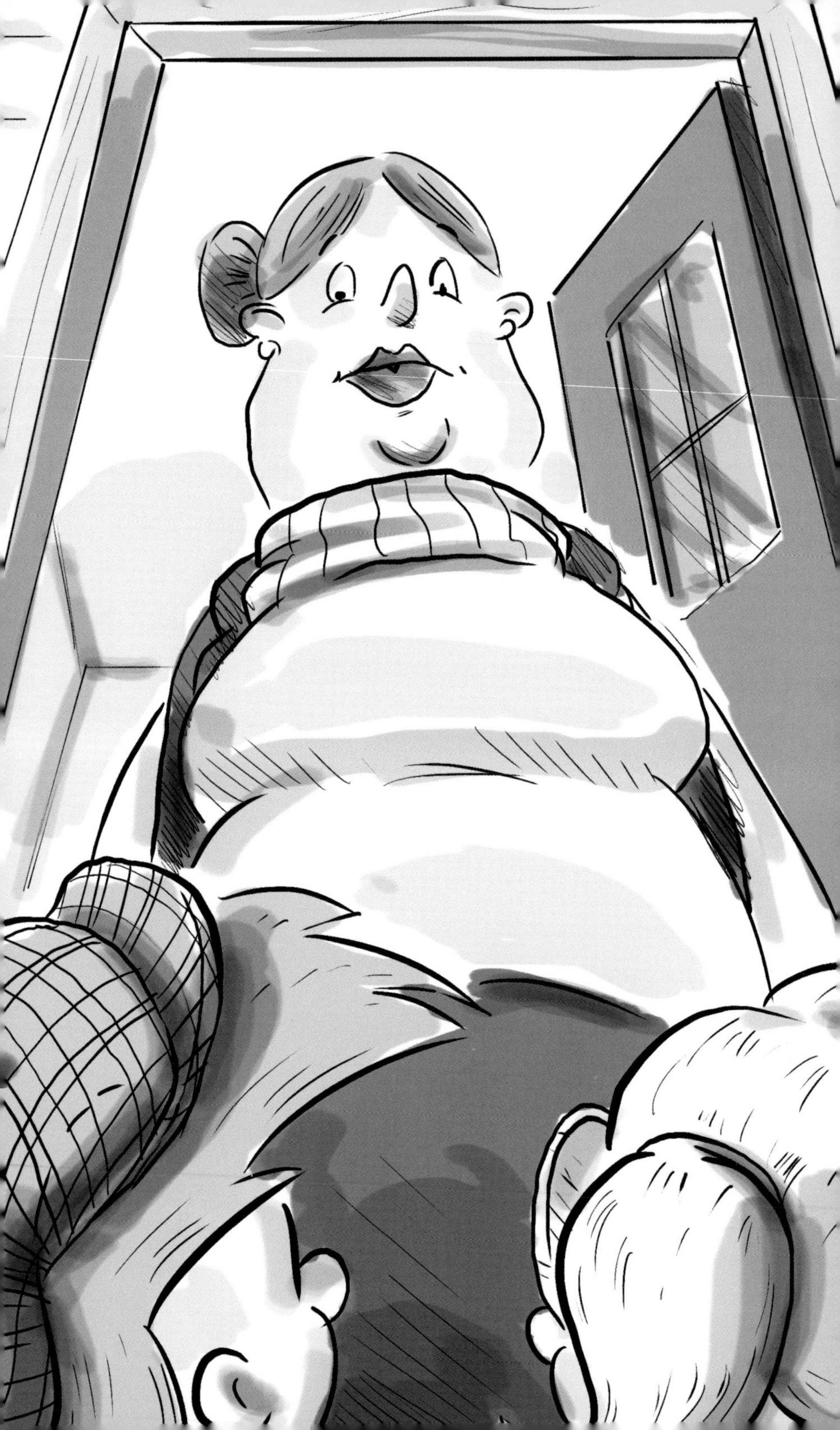

Chapter 7

In full costume, Kenny, Harriet, and I knocked on Mrs. Wiggins' front door. She answered and looked at us with a strange expression.

"Hello, Mrs. Wiggins. We are not here to talk about library books. We are here because we are journalists for our school newspaper and we are doing an investigation into the case of the missing elephant. Do you have time to talk to us?" I said.

"Sure, I do," she said. "What's the name of your school's paper? And why are you looking at me through that magnifying glass?"

I put the magnifying glass in my pocket. "It's called the, uh, the…" I didn't know what to say because, of course, the paper didn't exist.

"It's called *The Daily Mail*," Harriet said.

"You kids put out a paper every day?" Mrs. Wiggins said. "That's extraordinary."

"Well, it's just called that because it sounds good. Kind of like *The New York Times* tells you more than just what time it is in New York, but the name sounds good," Harriet said.

Mrs. Wiggins smiled. "Come on in, kids. I'm just cooking some dinner. There's my husband on the couch. Say hello to these reporters, Carl," she said.

Carl Wiggins was reading the newspaper in the living room. He lifted a hand and waved at us.

"Mr. Wiggins," I began. "Do you have any allergies?"

"Yeah, I do. I'm allergic to pollen and dust," he said.

"But you aren't allergic to peanuts, are you?" Harriet asked. She took out her make-up brush and was getting ready to dust for fingerprints. Kenny was taking notes on his pad.

"Nope. In fact, I love them," Mr. Wiggins said. Just then Mrs. Wiggins entered the living room with a big bowl of peanuts.

"AH HA!" I yelled. Mr. and Mrs. Wiggins both jumped. "What's the matter, Michael?" Mrs. Wiggins asked. "You nearly scared us to death."

"Ah, nothing. I just see you're holding a bowl of peanuts," I said.

"Yes, I am. My husband loves them. We go through so many bags of these you'd never even believe it. The supermarket was having a big sale on them. That's why earlier I bought as many bags as I could carry," Mrs. Wiggins said.

Kenny, Harriet, and I looked at each other and nodded. "Ok, that will be all, Mr. and Mrs. Wiggins," I said.

"We can scratch them off the list," I said, when we were on the sidewalk. "She's not feeding an elephant with those peanuts. She's feeding her husband."

"Yeah, and he shouldn't be having a snack before dinner." Kenny said. "That's not good nutrition."

"Now we have to focus on the next suspect, Mr. Smalls. He's a hunter so maybe he wanted a trophy. He's a prime suspect," I said, lifting the magnifying glass to my eye. "You guys look like bugs now!" I said. "Ha!"

"Michael, knock that off. We have to be serious investigators," Harriet said. "Kenny, I hope you're taking good notes. I've been dusting for prints."

Kenny said he had been, so we headed for the Smalls' house. Their daughter, Penelope, answered the door. She's in my sister Abby's grade. She told us she'd get her parents and to wait in the living room.

That living room was crazy! There were animal heads all over the place! Lions, tigers, leopards, and more. He must have hunted those animals. Then I noticed a blank space over the fireplace. There was a frame there but no animal head at all.

I whispered to Kenny and Harriet: "Maybe that's the space for the elephant's head!" Their eyes bugged out. All three of us were terrified.

"Hey kids!" a loud voice said.

We all screamed and fell off the sofa.

Mr. Smalls reached his hand out and helped us get back up onto the sofa.

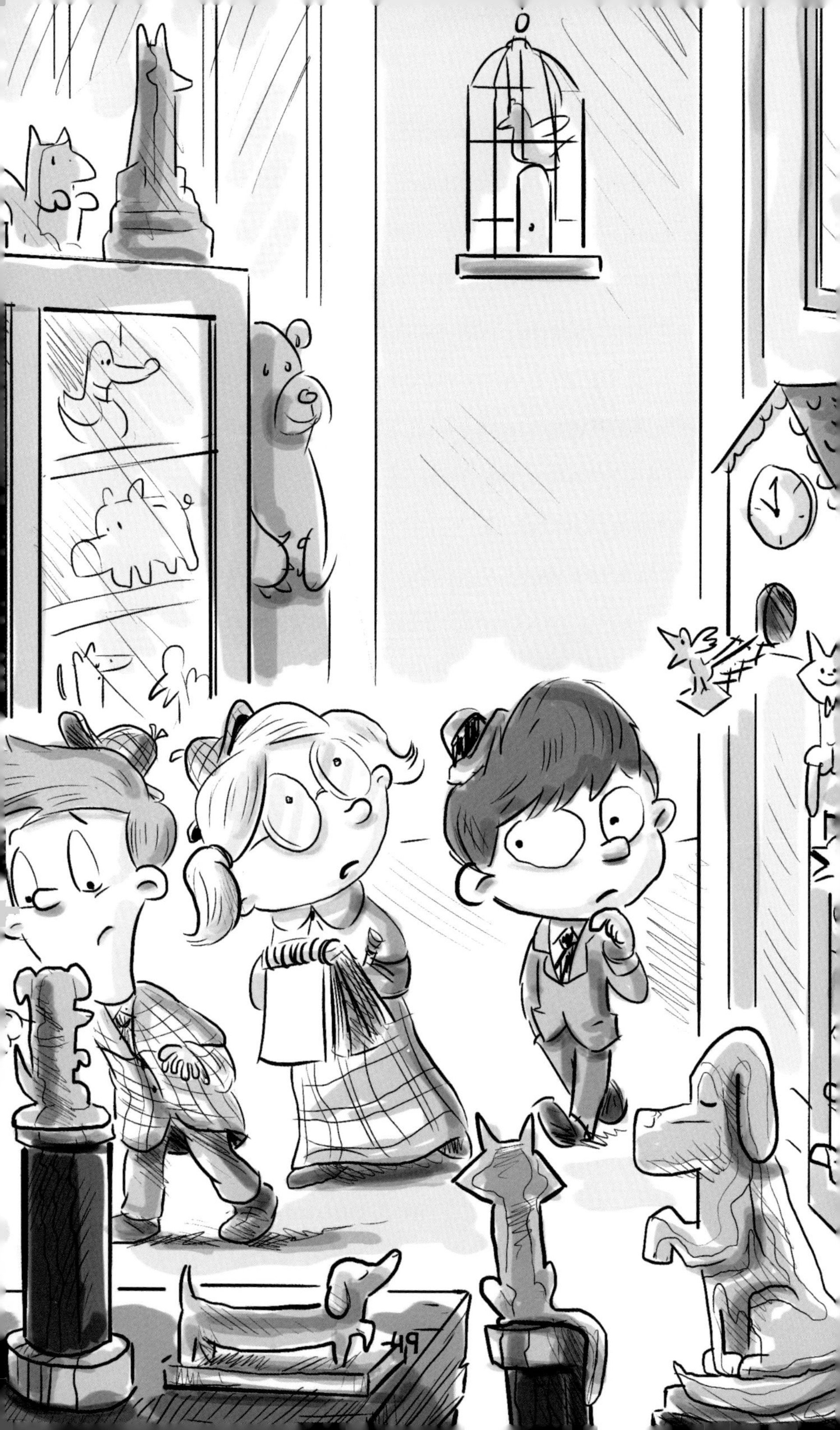

"Everything ok, kids?" he said.

"Mr. Smalls," Harriet said. "We are here with our school newspaper doing an investigation and we have a few questions for you."

"Sure, shoot," he said

Just then, Kenny screamed. "No, don't shoot! We're just innocent kids."

Mr. Smalls laughed. "I meant, you can ask me anything. Go for it."

"Where were you the other day when the elephant went missing?" Harriet asked, pacing back and forth."

"We were all home cleaning the house," he said.

"And what is going there on that wall?" I asked, pointing to the space above the fireplace with my magnifying glass. "Another animal head?"

"No, my wife is painting a family portrait. She's almost done."

"Ok, but there sure are a lot of animal heads here in your house. I guess you really like hunting," I said.

"I do from time to time, but only certain birds. These heads don't belong to animals I've killed.

I am an artist, like my wife, and I've sculpted and painted these animals. I'm delighted you think they're real!"

"I see," I said. "That will be all, Mr. Smalls."

On the sidewalk, the three of us huddled together.

"He could be lying!" Harriet said. "He did admit he hunts birds. How do we know he's telling the truth?"

"Yeah, and how do we know that the Wiggins family isn't lying, too? Maybe they knew we were onto them and that's why she served her husband those peanuts! The elephant can be in the basement for all we know," Kenny said.

"Well, now it's on to the last house," I said. And we all made our way to that big old abandoned house the rich kid's family was supposed to fix up. There were still cobwebs everywhere and the sun was setting, so it was kind of scary.

"We have to be home soon," Kenny said. "Don't forget that. I get extremely nervous when I break rules. You don't want me to start to panic, Michael!"

"I know. I've seen your nervous fits enough times," I said.

"But we have to investigate this last lead," Harriet said. "The elephant is counting on us!"

The three of us were slowly approaching the house when, all of a sudden, a light went on in one of the upstairs rooms.

We screamed.

"I am WAY too scared to go in there now, Mikey," Kenny said. "I need my inhaler. I can't breathe."

"It's true," I said. "A ghost or something even scarier could be in there!"

"Don't say that!" Kenny said.

We decided we had to go home. It wouldn't be safe to enter a house like that all alone. We'd have to find an adult and come back the next day.

If an adult was with us and we found the elephant in the house, I wouldn't get into trouble because everyone would be so happy the elephant was found. And if Erik tried to call the news to tell them I was responsilble, they wouldn't care because Jimmy already admitted he forgot to close the gate.

"But what would an elephant be doing turning on lights in an abandoned house?" Kenny asked after he calmed down.

"That's easy," Harriet said. "She'd be doing her hair and make-up. A girl needs the proper lighting to do that, you know."

Kenny and I just shrugged. We had to take her word for it.

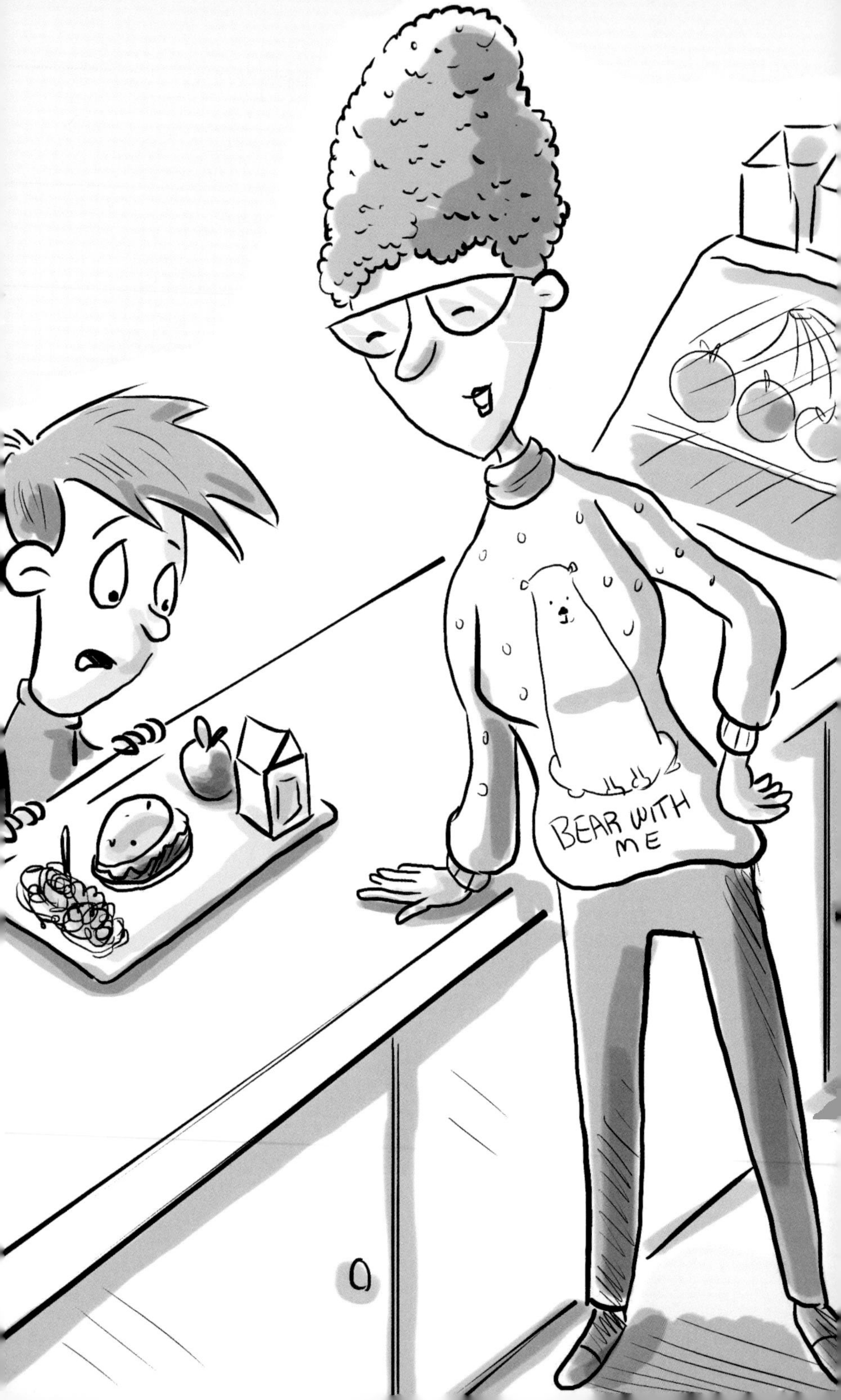
BEAR WITH ME

Chapter 8

The next day at school I was waiting in line for lunch, spacing out. I really was feeling guilty about the escaped elephant. I mean, where could she be? We had some leads, but she wasn't in any of those places, so now what? It's strange that an elephant can be missing for two days.

I took a look at the cafeteria menu. I wasn't very inspired by any of the choices.

"How's it goin', darlin'?" Ms. Fox said. No one outside of my family ever called me that and I liked it.

"I'm just not that excited about lunch today," I said.

"You don't like burgers?" she asked.

"Yeah, but I'm not all that hungry," I said.

"Well, you can always go with the salad or a deli sandwich! They don't disappoint!"

"You're right," I said. "Besides, I probably need to start making healthier food choices if I'm going to keep up with all of my activities!"

"That sounds like a smart decision!" Mrs. Fox said. "What activities are you into these days?"

I wanted to tell her about the elephant hunt, but I figured that would just lead to more trouble. "Oh, you know, the usual: biking, exploring, and all that kind of stuff."

"That sounds great! You just be sure to be safe! I love exploring the outdoors – you know I have a thing for wildlife! That's why I'm going to school at night to be a veterinarian!"

"Wow, Ms. Fox, I had no idea!" I said. "Oh, and I like your shirt," I added. There was a giant polar bear on it and below the bear were the words, "Bear with me, please."

"Well, thank you! Now you best keep moving in line, darlin'!" she said. So I thanked her and moved on.

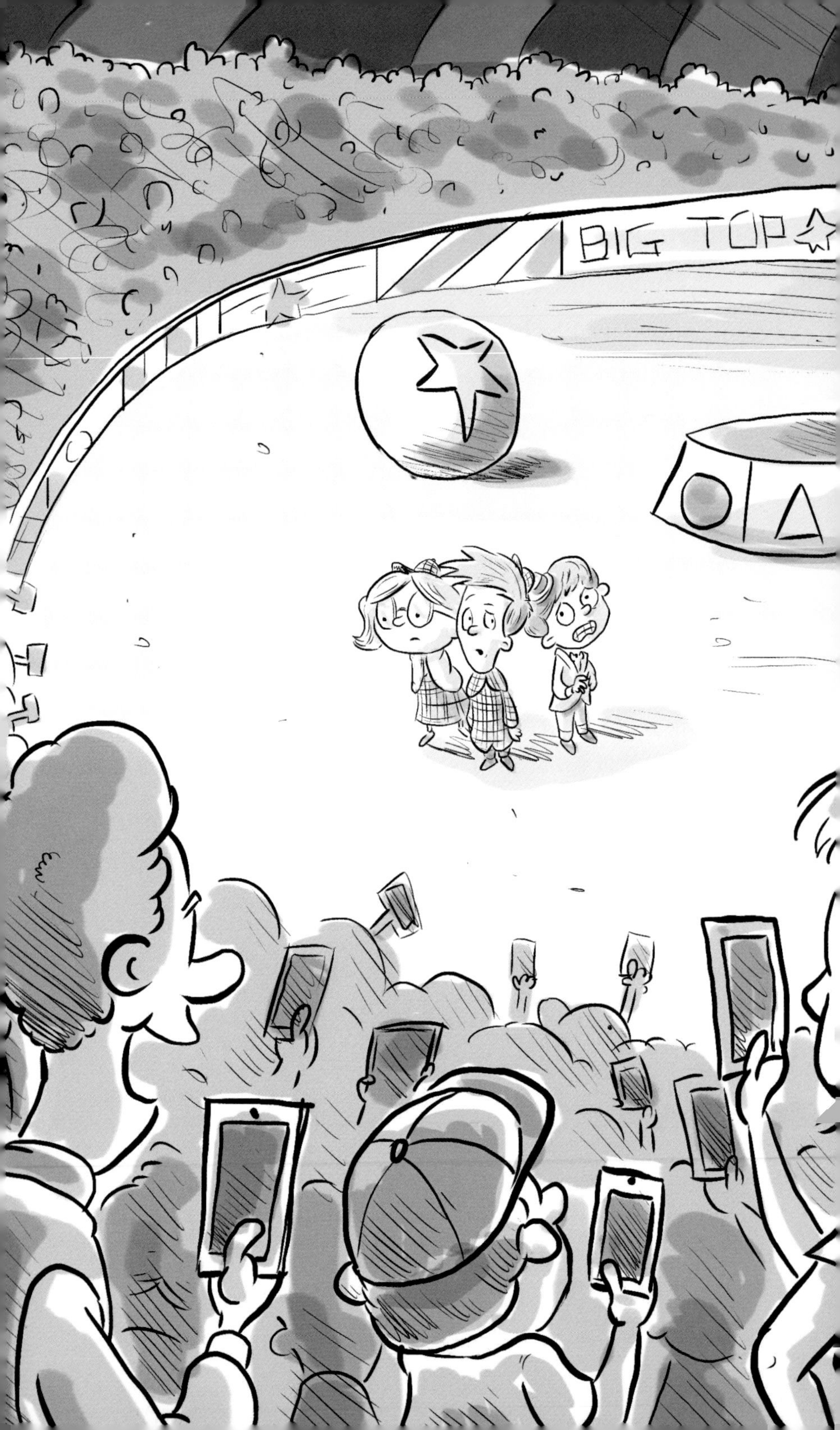
BIG TOP

Chapter 9

You know how sometimes ideas just come to you out of the blue?

That happens to me a lot. Some of the ideas are good and some are not so good, but the thing is they all seem really good at first.

I was just sitting there on my sofa thinking about my conversation with Ms. Fox when I remembered one of the kids in my school who was saying mean things about her the other day. He said that the circus is in town and he was right. It is! Maybe they needed another elephant or maybe she just saw a bunch of other elephants hanging around talking about peanuts and stuff and she just decided to join the circus? It could happen, I guess.

I called Harriet and Kenny. My mother said I could go over to Harriet's house after dinner.

We met at our command center, Harriet's basement, and dressed in our inspector costumes.

"Guys, how are we going to get to the circus without adults? We can't do that?" Kenny said. I could see he was nervous. His cheeks were all red and he was breathing really fast.

"I thought of that a little while ago when Michael called me," Harriet said, smiling. "I told my father that I wanted to get the ringmaster's autograph so he agreed to drive us and wait outside."

And he did! I was wondering if he'd get bored out there in the car waiting for us but he said we shouldn't worry. He'd just be on his phone the whole time.

The circus was awesome. **It was HUGE**, just like the supermarket but without food and three big rings and a really high ceiling. It hadn't started when we got there. People were still arriving and taking their seats. It was pretty dark though.

Then I got another idea. Remember I said that ideas always seem great when I get them? Well, this was another one.

"Hey, guys, let's just take a peek behind the tent and see if the elephant is there," I said.

Kenny and Harriet agreed.

"But, I'd better not get in trouble with the authorities," Harriet said. "I have my reputation to think of."

"Let's just get to it!" I said. I lifted the magnifying glass to my eye, Kenny took out his tiny note pad and pencil, and Harriet had out her make-up brush and powder. We were ready…

Over on the side we noticed a door that said PERFORMERS on it. We crept in that direction.

"The elephants must be in there getting ready," I said.

"But we're not allowed in," Kenny said. "We're not performers. And I think I need my inhaler, Mikey. This is getting stressful."

Just then a really big bald guy holding a walkie-talkie opened the door and said, "All right, let's go. Show's starting soon. Get ready!"

I guess he thought we were performers. But why would he think that? We're just normal kids in strange costumes.

We entered and saw acrobats, clowns, lion tamers and everyone else getting ready. They were putting on make-up, getting into their costumes and putting on wigs. It was great! They were laughing and everyone was so happy. Maybe I'll join a circus when I grow up.

Kenny, Harriet, and I huddled in the corner.

"Where are the animals?" I asked.

"Let's ask," Harriet said. She asked one of the acrobats who was wearing a really tight blue costume that made it look like he had blue skin. It gave me funny feelings to look at him. He told us the animals were behind the tent just a few feet away. The three of us made our way over there, lifted up the tent wall and saw about ten elephants!

"Jiminy Cricket!" I cried. "There she is!"

"Which one?" Kenny asked.

"Ah, good question," I said. "They kind of all look the same."

Then we heard a man's voice. "Ok, let's go, kids. It's show time!" It was the same big bald guy with the walkie-talkie.

Before we could say anything, he led us to the stage door. The next thing we knew the spotlights were shining on us as we marched out into the main ring with a bunch of acrobats, clowns, and other performers. The audience was clapping and holding up their cellphones to film us. Oh no! Now there's video to prove what we did.

We had no idea what to do so we just followed the clowns and acrobats. Some of them looked at us like they were a bit confused, but they found a use for us.

They threw balls and bowling pins at US

and I guess we were supposed to catch them. The problem was, of course, we didn't know how. The balls and pins kept coming at us and we dropped most of them, but the audience didn't mind. They were all cracking up. I guess they thought this was planned.

Then the acrobats took us by the hand and led us up to a high wire.

"I'm NOT walking on that thing!"

I said.

"Don't worry. We'll carry you," one of the acrobats said. And they did. Three acrobats held us as they rode their bikes across the high wire. The audience went wild. I made sure not to look down because it was far. But there was a net there so I wasn't really nervous.

After the high wire, a clown squeezed a flower on his jacket and squirted each of us in the face with water. The audience loved it! Then we found our way out of there and back outside.

Harriet's father was still looking at his cell phone in the car.

"Oh, that was fast," he said. "Did you get the ringmaster's autograph?"

"No, we didn't," Harriet said.

"And why are your faces wet?" he asked as we pulled away.

"A clown played a trick on us after we walked the high wire," Kenny said.

"Ha! You guys are so funny," Harriet's father said.

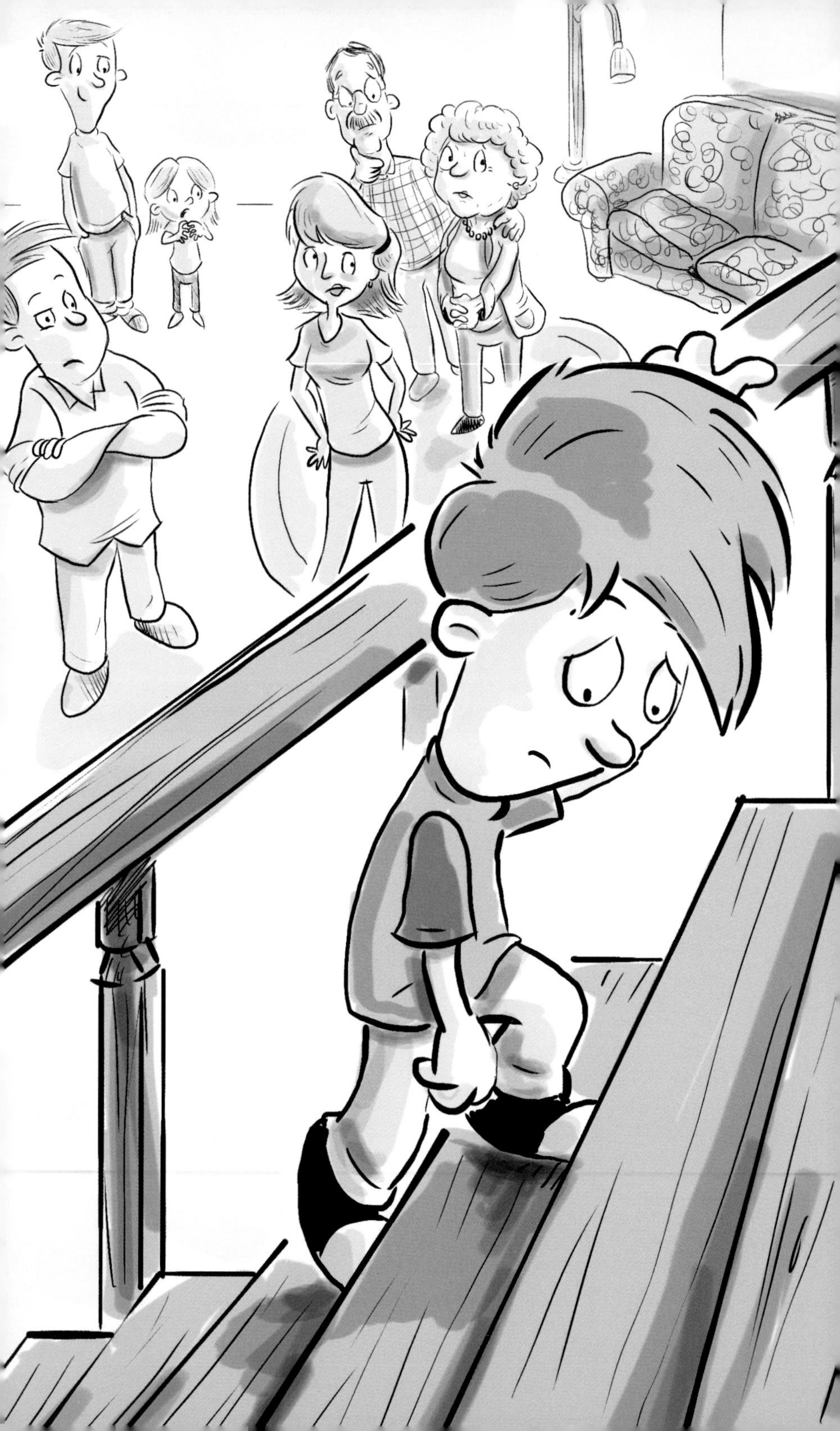

Chapter 10

When we left the circus I was super nervous because I thought we'd never find that elephant. To distract myself, I borrowed my mom's iPad, plopped onto the sofa in the family room and started playing CASTLES! I got really into it, as usual. It's fun when the colors change and the game bleeps and if you win a round a little guy pops up on the screen and screams, "You DID it!"

I lost track of time, but I knew dinner would be served soon. My grandparents were coming over and even though they are great old birds, I would rather just play all night long.

I was in the middle of a game when I got that

creepy sense that someone was looking at me. I paused the game and looked up from the screen and there was everyone in my family: my mother, father, brother, sister, and grandparents all staring at me like I was an animal at the zoo.

"Michael, we called you about ten times to come to the table. Why are you ignoring us?" my mother said.

"I wasn't ignoring you, Mom, really," I said. "I didn't even hear you."

"You didn't hear," my father said, "because you're so involved in that game. It's become an addiction Michael. I want you to start a 12-step program right now."

"What's that, Dad?" I asked.

"You walk up those 12 steps right there to the dining room and eat dinner with us. Hear me?" he said. "Now!"

"Ok, Dad. I'm sorry," I said.

In the middle of the meal (chicken parm, pasta, and broccoli, yum!) my grandmother asked where we thought the escaped elephant could possibly be.

I started to panic because I knew what I had to do. I had to admit what I did. I could feel my heart racing in my chest and my cheeks started to feel warm. I was so red, I must have looked like a giant tomato-head. I wondered if they knew I was the reason she had escaped from the zoo. Maybe Jimmy said something to his mother who told my mother? **I HATED feeling like this.** I needed a long bubble bath to calm my nerves.

"I think the elephant is in another zoo," my sister, Abby, said out of nowhere when she finished her chicken parm. "She probably didn't like that old one."

"Yeah," my brother, Joey, said. "And besides, Jimmy left the door open so she could escape in the first place. Who knows if maybe he sometimes forgot to feed her or wash her."

"Eww!" Abby cried. "She would smell so gross then."

"Ok, enough of that talk at the dinner table," my mother said.

I was still nervous. I just couldn't take it anymore, so I dropped to my knees next to my chair and said, "I have a confession, everyone. I have sinned!

I HAVE SINNED!"

"Michael, we're not at church," my father said. "Get up and tell us from your chair. We can't even see you down there."

"Oh," I said. "Sure."

Then I spilled my guts. It's the first time I ever did this. Normally I waited to get caught, but I couldn't take it anymore. I had to just say it.

"I am the one who is responsible for the elephant escaping. It's **ME, ME, ME!**" I said crying.

"How is that possible?" my mother asked. "You don't work at the zoo. You had nothing to do with it."

"I did, Mom, I did. I begged Jimmy Gorton to keep playing CASTLES! with me and he did." It felt so good to get that off my chest, but I felt dizzy for a moment as I waited for their reactions.

"What does that have to do with it?" my grandfather asked.

"If he wasn't playing that game he would have been paying attention to the elephants and they would never have escaped," I explained. I was relieved to say it, but I was still crying. "I even promised him I'd tell cousin Mary he was super nice, even to little kids. He kind of likes her."

"Michael," my father said, "it's really not your fault those elephants escaped that day. Jimmy should have said that he couldn't continue playing with you and that's that. If you're guilty of anything, it's that you were playing the game when you should have been looking at the animals and talking to your family. I should have taken my phone back sooner, then none of this would have happened. Next time I will. You have a problem with electronics and your mother and I are going to carefully monitor you from now on. We should never have let it get to this point and we're sorry for that. And, besides, your cousin does not need you to find boyfriends for her! She's dating a very nice young man in college now."

"You mean it's not my fault the elephants escaped that day?" I asked, wiping the tears from my eyes.

"Not really, Michael," my mother said. "It's mostly Jimmy's fault, and the zoo's for not having backup safety measures. But in the future, you shouldn't distract people when they're at work. Let them just do their jobs, all right?"

"Ok, Mom, I will." I felt so good. Phew. I thought I was going to go to zoo-jail like the rest of the animals behind the bars. And you know what? I felt good about myself for finally **- FOR THE FIRST TIME -** admitting that I did something wrong BEFORE I got caught.

I thought I deserved some pizza for that. I also wanted to tell them I disobeyed them and rode my bike twice really far, but I just couldn't do it then. I was exhausted.

At the end of the night, after my grandparents went home, my family and I were watching the news on TV when the reporter said something that made us all jump off the sofa: "This just in: The elephant that had been missing from the zoo for the past three days has been found alive and well!"

YAY!

We were all SO happy, we were high-fiving each other and cheering.

Then the reporter interviewed the zookeeper and the chief of police. The zookeeper said the elephant was returned in even better condition than if she had been in the zoo. Just then the reporter interviewed that citizen.

You're never going to believe who it was... It was Ms. Fox, the lunch lady!

She said, "Earlier this evening I went out back to our barn to check on something when, lo and behold, I saw an elephant resting on a bale of hay. I thought I was hallucinating because that runs in my family—on my father's side, right, Mama? **But I wasn't hallucinating! It really WAS an elephant, live in the flesh in my barn.**

She must have been there all week, munching on the hay and drinking water from the leaky hose."

Ms. Fox continued after taking a sip of water, "Many of you don't know this, but I've been going to night school for quite a while now and very soon I will be a licensed veterinarian, so I know very well how to take care of an animal. I did a quick examination of her health and then immediately called the authorities."

My brother, sister, father, mother and I all said, "Wow!" at the same time.

"What an amazing story!" my mother said and we all agreed.

At first, I thought it was Jimmy Gorton, the Wiggins, the Smalls, or even the circus. But I **NEVER EVER** suspected it was no one, that the elephant spent the three days chilling in a barn all by herself!

Sometimes it's really hard to figure out the ending.

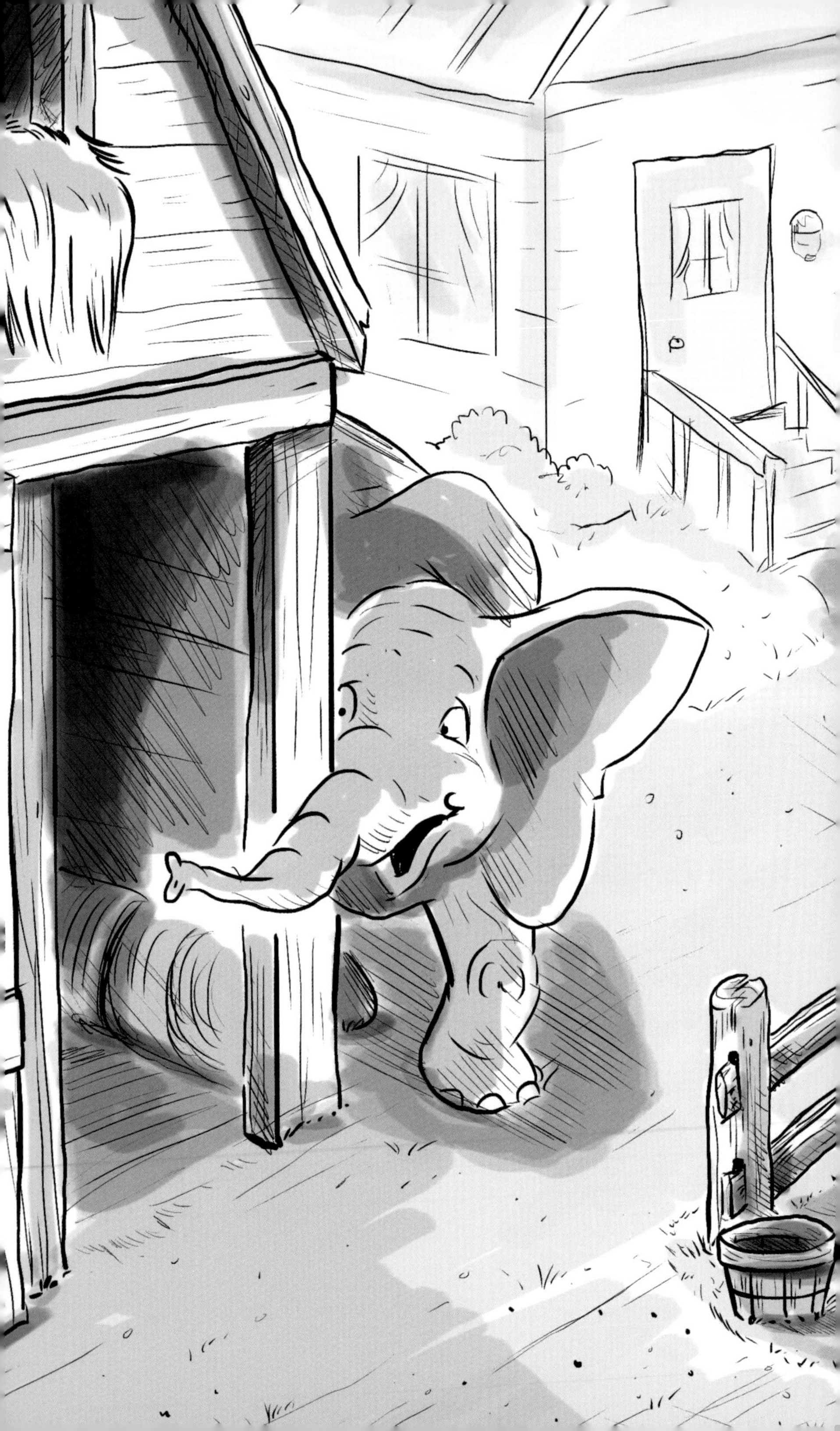

Chapter 11

At school the next day everyone wanted to talk to Ms. Fox. It was like she was a celebrity or the person who invented pizza or something. She said she'd only be working at my school for another few weeks because then she'd become a full-time veterinarian.

But there was still one issue remaining. I had to tell my parents I disobeyed them twice and rode my bike far, to the other end of town, without their permission.

I waited until after dinner that night to tell them.

"Mom, Dad, I have something to confess," I said.

"Oh, no, what now?" my mother asked. She did not look happy.

My father closed his eyes and started to rub the sides of his head.

"Remember when you told me not to ride my bike far and to stay close to the house? Well, I didn't listen. I rode to the other side of town to go to the Carter farm when you told me not to go more than two blocks away," I said.

"Why did you do that? What got into you?" my father said.

"Well, my friends and I thought we'd find the elephant there. And, as you know, I thought it was my fault she escaped in the first place so I thought I HAD to find her no matter what. Plus, I was worried that Erik, that fifth grader, might know the whole story and would tell on me." My mother asked, "Why did you think Erik was going to tell on you?" "He smirked at me in the locker room," I said. My mother rolled her eyes.

"So that means you were also trespassing on Farmer Carter's property, too," my mother said.

"Yes, it does, I'm sorry," I said. And I was sorry. Really, I was.

"Trespassing is wrong and it can be extremely dangerous, Michael. You do realize you have earned some consequences now. We will tell you later exactly what those consequences will be," my father said.

"But, Michael, I do think it's commendable you admitted on your own that you did these things," my mother said. "And although you still make mistakes, it appears you are learning."

"What does commendable mean, Mom?" I asked.

"It means worthy of praise. Now promise both of us you won't leave the area without our permission and you won't trespass on anyone's property ever again," my mother said.

"And no more lies. I thought we already went over this in the past," my father said.

"I promise, Dad. Really… Well, there is one more thing. I did kind of join a circus for a little while, but that's over now." I explained what happened to my parents and they said they'd call Kenny and Harriet's parents to make sure they knew what happened, too.

I also had to call Farmer Carter and apologize to him for trespassing on his property. He was not happy but thanked me for telling him.

As usual, my whole family spent time together talking in the living room at the end of the night for a little while. We talked about respecting yourself by eating well, working hard, and not overusing technology.

My mother said, in the future, whenever my brother, sister, or I can't seem to do those things, to ask a trusted adult like a teacher or a family member for some help. No one is perfect, and there's nothing wrong with asking for assistance.

"Technology is certainly very appealing," my mother said. "There's always a game to play or a posting to check, but most things are best done in moderation. Try to limit your use of technology to a maximum of one or two hours per day and I'll do the same. Many adults have the same problem, too. We all need to spend less time in front of a screen and more time with other people."

We also talked about respecting others by not lying, teasing, trespassing on their property, or making fun of or threatening them. But, also, by doing what's right, including being honest, trustworthy, and kind.

My father said that we usually know what's right because of the way we feel when doing something or even thinking about it. He asked me how I felt trespassing on Farmer Carter's property and I said I was super nervous and didn't want to do it.

"That's right, Michael," he said. "Being nervous was a good clue that you were doing the wrong thing. And, like your mother said, if you're not sure, ask a trusted adult for help. Another rule to use is: Ask yourself how you'd feel if someone did the action you're considering to you or to someone you love. If the answer is that you wouldn't like it, don't do it."

Joey, Abby, and I all agreed that that was good advice. My parents said they would remind us from time to time because it's easy to forget things you learn.

Then we all went into the dining room for dessert.

I grabbed the iPad to play after we were done eating.

My mother had baked elephant ear cookies the day before. They are buttery and delicious with a nice sugar coating.

We each got one cookie with a large glass of milk and we talked more about the escaped elephant and how happy we were that she was finally found, safe and sound, and returned to the zoo. My mother said she wondered how a whole three days could go by without Ms. Fox hearing the elephant in her barn. "I mean, it's possible, but it's also possible she was taking care of her the whole time, waiting for the zoo to get its act together before bringing her back," she said. "The zoo did announce they were retraining their employees and doing more safety checks. Well, Ms. Fox certainly knows what she's doing. But, who knows? At least it's over and the elephant is safe."

But I still had a couple of questions. One was about how the elephant got to Ms. Fox's house when the police said she was last seen on a different street. My father said the back of Ms. Fox's property was actually very close to Pine Drive. Kenny, Harriet, and I were really very close! If only we looked a bit farther we probably would have found the elephant.

There was still one more thing I was
wondering. "You know that old abandoned
house on Pine Drive?" I said to my
parents. "You know that I saw a
light go on at night. That's scary
right? Maybe there's a ghost
in there or something."

"Michael, that light is on a timer," my mother said. "The real estate agency put it there so the house wouldn't look so uninviting."

Mystery solved! Phew. A timer is better than a ghost, that's for sure.

Even though Kenny, Harriet, and I didn't solve the case. I think we make a good team. Maybe we'll do another investigation together soon.

I'm also glad I'm finally getting along with Harriet. She's odd, for sure, but everyone is in some way or another.

As soon as I finished my elephant ear, I opened the CASTLES! app to see if I could beat my all-time high score. But while I was logging in, I thought, I have a choice: I can play this game or talk to my family some more.

I turned the iPad off, put it

away in the kitchen drawer, and returned to my seat in the dining room.

I decided to spend more time with my family because we usually have a lot of fun together.

We talked and laughed for the rest of the night. My father even made a few silly elephant jokes. I would have missed all of this if I was playing video games instead.

"What do you call an elephant that doesn't matter?... *An irrelephant!*"

"What's big, gray, and wears glass slippers?... *Cinderelephant!*"

"Dad, enough!" my brother, sister and I all said at the same time.

"Ok, just one more!" he said. "What do you get when you cross a potato with an elephant?... *Mashed potatoes!*"

I made the right choice, didn't I?

Tips & Questions

"I turned the iPad off, put it away
in the kitchen drawer, and returned
to my seat in the dining room.
I decided to spend more time with
my family because we usually have
a lot of fun together."

– Michael McMichaels

"There's always a game to play or a posting to
check, but most things are best done in moderation."
– Michael's Mother

Michael learned what can happen if you distract someone
from what they are supposed to be doing. He also learned that
paying too much attention to technology can take away from
real life experiences. Take a look at some of these examples and
discuss what is the best choice, or solution.

1. **DISCUSS** - Why is it important to listen to trusted adults
and not lie to them about what you're doing and where
you're going?

2. **SHARE** - Did you ever get in trouble for lying to your
parents or a teacher? Why did you lie? What happened as
a result?

3. **DISCUSS/SHARE** - Why is it important not to distract
people when they are working? Did you ever make a
mistake because someone distracted you? What happened?

4. **DISCUSS/SHARE** - Why is moderation important? What
area of your life other than technology use can benefit
from more moderation?

5. **SHARE** - How much time per day do you think is too much for most people to spend using technology? Do you spend too much time on a phone, computer, or tablet, or in front of the TV?

6. **ADULTS DISCUSS** - What can you do to limit the amount of time children spend in front of one screen or another?

7. **DISCUSS/TRY** - What alternatives to using technology can you think of? Make a list and attach it to the refrigerator. Every time someone in the family does one of those things instead of using technology, put a star next to his/her name. Whoever has the most stars at the end of the month should get a prize, such as a book, or get to pick the next family outing.

8. **DISCUSS** - Why is it important to limit the use of technology when others are around? Define politeness. What role does it play in using technology when others are around?

9. **SHARE/DISCUSS** - Do you have a pet? How much time per day do you spend together? Who makes sure he/she is fed and taken care of properly? What other things do you do for your pet that ensure he/she is as happy and healthy as possible?

10. **DISCUSS** - In this book, Ms. Fox is judged based on how she looks/what she wears. Why is it important not to judge people that way? Has that ever happened to you? How did it make you feel?

Critics LOVE this series!

978-1-934490-94-5

978-1-944882-03-7

978-1-944882-10-5

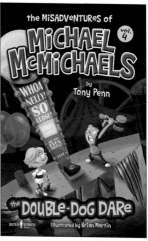

978-1-944882-21-1

"This is definitely a series you don't want to miss out on... Parents of elementary school-aged children, I highly recommend this series, this book, to you and your kids. Something you guys can read together. It's got a great narrative. It's right up there with 'Diaries of a Wimpy Kid' and 'The Dork Diaries'."

– Erin Wise, blogger, The Nerdy Girl Express

"Tony Penn is at it again, with yet another wonderful adventure for the mischievous, funny, heart-warming Michael McMichaels... Michael is every curious child (a Curious George, a Dennis the Menace) who never looks for trouble, yet it somehow finds him. Why? Michael is a character who is absolutely interested in everything going on around him, and for this reason he is authentically child-like, so real that every reader will want to hug him, kiss him, follow the frivolity of his story and ask Tony Penn to fill us with more adventures, so we can discover what trouble Michael will get into in the next volume. Fun, heart-warming and so well-written, I would recommend this for all young boys, and for the girls, too!"

– P. L. Laskin, book reviewer

Boys Town Press
Featured Titles

Kid-friendly books to teach social skills

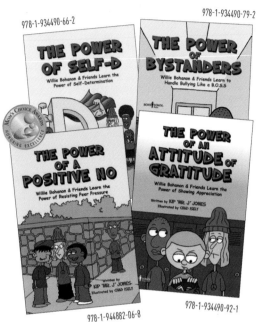

978-1-934490-66-2

978-1-934490-79-2

978-1-944882-06-8

978-1-934490-92-1

978-1-944882-21-1

978-1-944882-10-

978-1-944882-03-7

978-1-934490-94-5

978-1-934490-54-9

978-1-934490-60-0

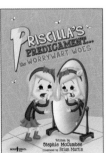

978-1-934490-87-7

978-1-934490-77-8

BOYS TOWN®
Press

BoysTownPress.org

For information on Boys Town, its Education Model®, Common Sense Parenting®, and training programs:
boystowntraining.org , boystown.org/parenting
EMAIL: training@BoysTown.org, PHONE: 1-800-545-5771

For parenting and educational books and other resources:
BoysTownPress.org, EMAIL: btpress@BoysTown.org, PHONE: 1-800-282-6657